COPY 1

j398.2   Zemach, H.
Zemac   Mommy, buy me
1975   a china doll.

795

COPY 1

795

j398.2   Zemach, Harve.
Zemac   Mommy, buy me a china doll : adapted from
1975   an Ozark children's song / by Harve Zemach ;
         pictures by Margot Zemach. New ed. New York
         : Farrar, Straus, Giroux, 1975.
             1 v. (unpaged) : ill.

I. Title.
0374350051 1b   0036889 LC

39   INV 85

MOMMY, BUY ME A CHINA DOLL

MOMMY, BUY ME A CHINA DOLL

Adapted from an Ozark children's song by

HARVE ZEMACH

Pictures by MARGOT ZEMACH

FARRAR · STRAUS · GIROUX · NEW YORK

Mommy, buy me a china doll,
Do, Mommy, do!
What could we buy it with, Eliza Lou?

We could trade our Daddy's featherbed,
Do, Mommy, do!

Trade our Daddy's featherbed?

Then where would our Daddy sleep, Eliza Lou?

He could sleep in the horsey's bed,
Do, Mommy, do!
Trade our Daddy's featherbed,
Daddy in the horsey's bed—
Then where would our horsey sleep, Eliza Lou?

He could sleep in our Sister's bed
For a day or two.
Trade our Daddy's featherbed,
Daddy in the horsey's bed,
Horsey in our Sister's bed—
Then where would our Sister sleep, Eliza Lou?

She could sleep in the baby's bed,
Do, Mommy, do!
Trade our Daddy's featherbed,
Daddy in the horsey's bed,
Horsey in our Sister's bed,
Sister in the baby's bed—
Then where would the baby sleep, Eliza Lou?

He could sleep in the kittens' bed,
Do, Mommy, do!
Trade our Daddy's featherbed,
Daddy in the horsey's bed,
Horsey in our Sister's bed,
Sister in the baby's bed,
Baby in the kittens' bed—
Then where would our kittens play, Eliza Lou?

They could play in the chicken coop,
Do, Mommy, do!
Trade our Daddy's featherbed,
Daddy in the horsey's bed,
Horsey in our Sister's bed,
Sister in the baby's bed,
Baby in the kittens' bed,
Kittens in the chicken coop—
Then where would the chickens roost, Eliza Lou?

They could roost on Granny's rocking chair,

Do, Mommy, do!

Trade our Daddy's featherbed,

Daddy in the horsey's bed,

Horsey in our Sister's bed,

Sister in the baby's bed,

Baby in the kittens' bed,

Kittens in the chicken coop,

Chickens on the rocking chair—

Then where would Granny sit and sew, Eliza Lou?

She could sit and sew in the piggy pen
Just for a day or two.
Trade our Daddy's featherbed,
Daddy in the horsey's bed,
Horsey in our Sister's bed,
Sister in the baby's bed,
Baby in the kittens' bed,
Kittens in the chicken coop,
Chickens on the rocking chair,
Granny in the piggy pen—
Then where would our piggies go, Eliza Lou?

We could let them stay in my own bed,
Do, Mommy, do!
Trade our Daddy's featherbed,
Daddy in the horsey's bed,
Horsey in our Sister's bed,
Sister in the baby's bed,
Baby in the kittens' bed,
Kittens in the chicken coop,
Chickens on the rocking chair,
Granny in the piggy pen,
Piggies in Eliza's bed—
Then where would Eliza sleep, Eliza Lou?

She could sleep on our Mommy's lap,
Do, Mommy, do!
Trade our Daddy's featherbed,
Daddy in the horsey's bed,
Horsey in our Sister's bed,
Sister in the baby's bed,
Baby in the kittens' bed,
Kittens in the chicken coop,
Chickens on the rocking chair,
Granny in the piggy pen,

Piggies in Eliza's bed,
Eliza on her Mommy's lap,
Sleeping on her Mommy's lap,
Dreaming 'bout a china doll,
Sleep, Eliza Lou.